Smelly Slugsy

Created by Keith Chapman

First published in Great Britain by HarperCollins Children's Books in 2005

1 3 5 7 9 10 8 6 4 2 ISBN: 0-00-720161-3

A CIP catalogue record for this title is available from the British Library.

Based on the television series *Fifi and the Flowertots* and the
original script 'Smelly Slugsy' by Diane Redmond
Special thanks to Cosgrove Hall Films
© Chapman Entertainment Limited 2005

Printed and bound in China

Smelly Slugsy

One sunny day, Fifi Forget-Me-Not was picking flowers to make potpourri for her friend, Poppy.

"I love potpourri!"

Fifi said to herself. Just then, Bumble buzzed into the garden. "What's potty poorly, Fifi?" he asked.

Fifi giggled. "Potpourri! It's a
mixture of herbs and flower petals
that smell nice and fresh."
"Mmm, smells lovely, Fifi," said Bumble.
"I just dropped by to tell you I heard Violet
and Primrose quarrelling just now."

"Buttercups and daisies,
not again!"

Fifi said, "I'd
better get over
there right
away!"

As Fifi arrived at Flowertot Cottage,
she heard lots of shouting.
"Don't my bowls look nicer on the windowsill, Fifi?"
asked Primrose.
"Or do you prefer them on the table?"
asked Violet.
"The windowsill is perfect!"
said Primrose.
"The table is better!" protested Violet.

"I think what you put **in** the bowls
is more important," said Fifi.
The two Tots continued to bicker
as the front door opened.

"Would you like to ssshare my cauliflower tonight?"
asked Slugsy shyly.
"No! Sorry Slugsy, I can't. I'm,
er, washing my petals!"
she stammered.
"But I've taken all of the
maggots out
of the
cauliflower
for you!"
Slugsy said.
**"Maggots?
Yuck!"**
said the
Flowertots.

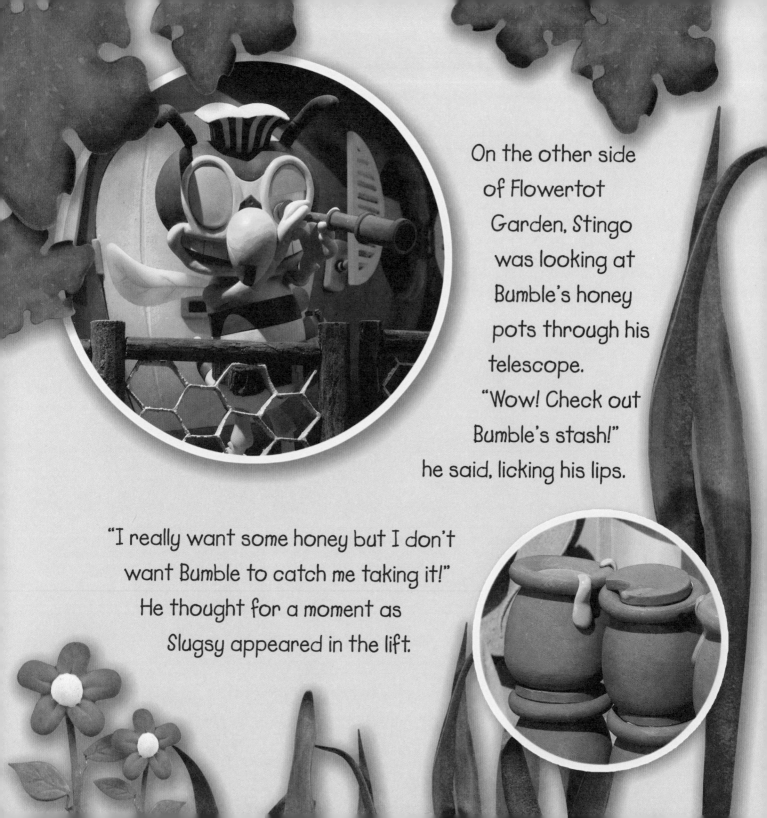

On the other side of Flowertot Garden, Stingo was looking at Bumble's honey pots through his telescope.
"Wow! Check out Bumble's stash!" he said, licking his lips.

"I really want some honey but I don't want Bumble to catch me taking it!" He thought for a moment as Slugsy appeared in the lift.

"I don't think Primrose likes me,
Ssstingo," said Slugsy sadly.
"Of course she doesn't like you!"
exclaimed Stingo, "you're a smelly slug!"
"Then how can I make myself sssmell nicer?"
Slugsy asked his pal.
Stingo smiled and threw his arm around Slugsy.
"How about a shower in something
sweet and runny?" he suggested.

Soon, Stingo and Slugsy were
sneaking into Bumble's garden.
"I don't think we ssshould be
in here," Slugsy said as
Stingo flipped open a pot
of honey and poured it all
over Slugsy's back!

"Bumble won't mind his old pal Stingo helping himself,"
Stingo muttered in between helping himself
to big yummy handfuls of honey.
"Mmm, it's so sweet," said Stingo.
"Eurgh, it's so sssticky!" Slugsy complained.
"I'm going to wash this off."
He slithered out of the garden,

leaving a long, sticky trail of honey behind him.

"Spoilsport Slugsy!"
called Stingo.

Back in the garden, Bumble **buzzed** over Fifi's gate.

"Oh, Fifi," he said, "one of my best pots of honey has disappeared. If I help you pick some lavender for Poppy's potpourri, would you please look for my honey?"

"Oh alright then," she agreed. "I'll also need lots of..."

"Oh Fiddly Flowerpetals,
I forgot!" laughed Fifi.
"Ha-ha!" smiled Bumble
"Fifi Forget-Me-Not forgot!"
"They begin with 'r' and grow on bushes...
They have thorns and smell lovely..."
Bumble tried to guess.
"Rhubarb?
Raspberries?
Rhododendrons?"
"No, no, no..." Fifi said.

"It's roses!"

Bumble got to work while Fifi skipped over to his garden and searched for clues. "Ah-ha!" she cried. "A slimy honey slug trail. There's only one slug in Flowertot Garden

and that's Slugsy! He must have taken Bumble's honey."

Fifi began to follow the honey trail.........

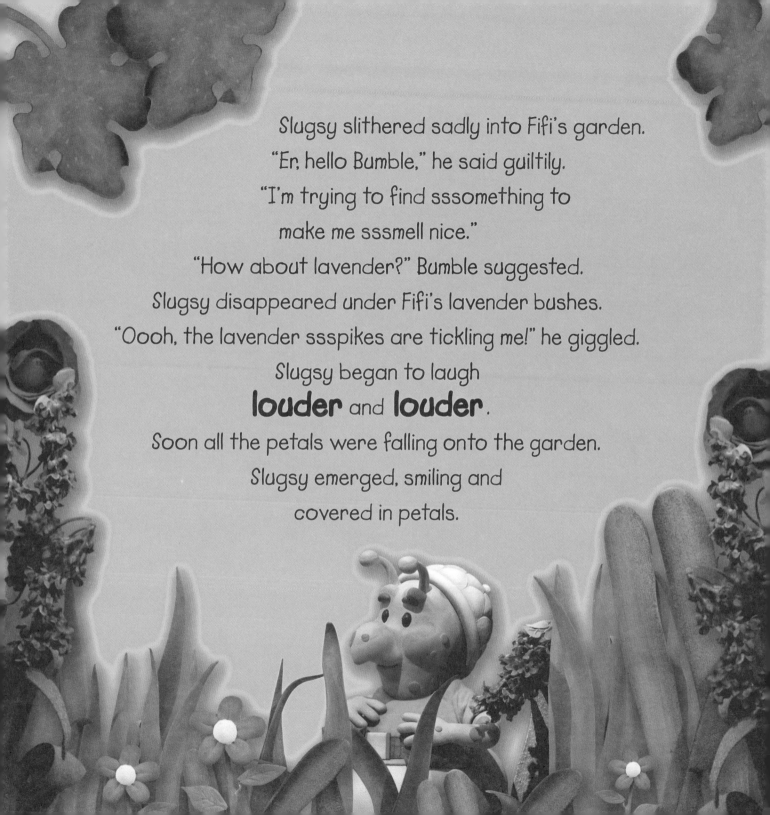

Slugsy slithered sadly into Fifi's garden.

"Er, hello Bumble," he said guiltily.

"I'm trying to find sssomething to
make me sssmell nice."

"How about lavender?" Bumble suggested.

Slugsy disappeared under Fifi's lavender bushes.

"Oooh, the lavender ssspikes are tickling me!" he giggled.

Slugsy began to laugh
louder and **louder**.

Soon all the petals were falling onto the garden.

Slugsy emerged, smiling and
covered in petals.

Fifi followed Slugsy's trail all the way back to her
garden. "You picked those quickly, Bumble!"
she said, spotting the piles of roses
and lavender petals.
"It wasn't me, Fifi!" he laughed,
pointing to
Slugsy.

"Just the slug I'm looking for,"
Fifi said firmly.
"It wasn't me that took the honey!
It was Ssstingo!"
Slugsy blurted out.
"Stingo shouldn't take things from
other people's gardens," said Fifi.
"He's a naughty, naughty
wasssp!" Slugsy agreed.
"Diddly Dandelions"
exclaimed Fifi.
"Look at the time! I've
got to get this potpourri
to Poppy!"
"Can I help you, Fifi?"
asked Slugsy kindly.

The friends had just finished packing the potpourri
into little baskets when they heard a buzzing sound.
It was Stingo, looking for Slugsy.
"Who said you could steal a pot of Bumble's best honey?"
asked Fifi sternly.

"It was for smelly Slugsy!" Stingo protested.
"You took the honey for yourself
and then tried to blame Slugsy!"
said Fifi.
"I think you should apologise, Stingo."
Stingo looked very cross.
"Sorry, Bumble," he said.
Fifi gave Slugsy a
basket of
potpourri.
"This is to make
your house smell
nice," she said.
"I've got a much
better idea!" said Slugsy.

"I've got a present for you, Primrose," Slugsy said.

"I hope it's not cauliflower," she said, taking the basket.

"Potpourri!
Slugsy, you're a genius, this is just what I need for my new bowls." Slugsy blinked in amazement, then smiled.

"Are you sure you won't come and ssshare my cauliflower cheese?" he asked.

"Oh all right, but I'll have to wear a peg on my nose," Primrose said.

"Is it me?" asked Slugsy, ashamed.

"Oh no!" exclaimed Primrose. "I just **hate** the smell of cauliflower!"

How To Make Your Own Smelly Socks

Hello there! Most people think that smelly socks aren't very nice but these ones smell lovely!

To make two Smelly Socks, you will need:

* Two clean socks
* Lavender or
* Potpourri (like the potpourri I made for Poppy!)
* 20cm of pretty ribbon per sock
* Extra ribbon for hanging

1. Make sure your socks are lovely and clean (new ones are best!)

2. Fill the sock with lavender or potpourri until it looks like it has a foot in it! Leave five centimetres empty at the top .

3. Tie the top of your sock with the ribbon, making sure it is fastened tightly, in a bow.

'We like to keep our smelly socks in our drawers to make our clothes smell nice. Sometimes we hang them in the wardrobe to keep our dresses fresh!'

Fifi and the Flowertots

Talking Fifi Forget-Me-Not. Own your very own scented Fifi! Fifi says 7 phrases and loves to be cuddled!

Have even more Flowertot fun with these Fifi activity books!

Fifi's Talent Show is available to buy on DVD and video now!

Includes five exciting stories!

Forget-Me-Not Cottage. Deluxe 30 piece playset including 6 scented characters! With flying Bumble, garden swing, flower ring, hair slide & lots more!

As seen on TV milkshake!

As seen on NICK Join In TV